# The Woolgatherer

## A Play in Two Acts

by William Mastrosimone

A SAMUEL FRENCH ACTING EDITION

SAMUEL FRENCH

FOUNDED 1830

New York  Hollywood  London  Toronto

SAMUELFRENCH.COM

THE WOOLGATHERER by William Mastrosimone was first performed by the Rutgers Theatre Company, New Brunswick, N.J. in July, 1979. The play was directed by John Bettenbender, Set by Joseph Miklojcik, Costumes by Vicki Rita McLaughlin, Stage Managed by Carol Hawk.

CLIFF ............................ *Ray Baker*

ROSE ....................... *Mary Beth Fisher*

The second professional production was presented at the Circle Rep, New York City in May, 1980. The play was directed by John Bettenbender, Set by Karl Egstei, and Lights by Dennis Parichy, Costumes by Joan E. Weiss, Stage Managed by Jody Boese, with the following cast:

CLIFF ........................... *Peter Weller*

ROSE .......................... *Patricia Wettig*

DEDICATION
To Carole Brigantine Shambora, I think

TIME: Now

PLACE: South Philadelphia

SET: Efficiency apartment.
    A single bed, neatly made.
    A small table.
    A chair.
    An orange crate.
    A door leading to a hallway.
    A closet.
    A boarded-up window hidden by cheap curtains.

## CAST

### ROSE

### CLIFF

# IMPORTANT BILLING AND CREDIT REQUIREMENTS

# THE WOOLGATHERER
## ACT ONE

*Darkness. Footfalls in the hallway. Inaudible talking. Lights up slowly. Keys fumbling in the doorlock. Enter ROSE followed by CLIFF swinging a sixpack in a paper-bag.*

ROSE. And there was this girl ... She was a poet ... And she lived here ... In this room ... Before, you know, I moved in ... And she committed, you know, suicide, right here in this room.

CLIFF. Did she die?

ROSE. Of course she died.

CLIFF. How'd she do it?

ROSE. Rope.

CLIFF. Overdose of rope?

ROSE. No. She, you know, hung herself.

CLIFF. Just kidding.

ROSE. That's not funny.

CLIFF. So why'd she do it?

ROSE. Nobody knows. It's a big mystery.

CLIFF. Big mystery. Didn't she leave a note?

ROSE. No. She left a poem.

CLIFF. Lucky she was a poet.

ROSE. Why's that?

CLIFF. Suppose she was a novelist.

ROSE. This is it. The poem she left. It's called "Death is my lover."

CLIFF. Beautiful.

ROSE. Want to hear it?

CLIFF. Yeah. Just what I need. Something to lift my spirits.

5

ROSE.

"Death is my lover,
You say it's not right,
But his love's forever
Day and night, day and night.
We've gone to elope,
Away from the light
In his cozy house,
Day and night, day and night.
So I go with equanimity—"

CLIFF. Go with who?

ROSE.

"So I go with equanimity,
Without a fight,
To be in his arms—"

CLIFF. Hey, hey, whoa, whoa. Look, kid, I had a rough day and I don't want to hear about no weirdo's suicide note.

ROSE. O, you don't like poetry?

CLIFF. Hey, I'm nuts about it.

ROSE. Really?

CLIFF. Hey.

ROSE. Do you write poetry?

CLIFF. Hey, everyday.

ROSE. Really?

CLIFF. Hey.

ROSE. I'd like to read some.

CLIFF. I don't write it down. I talk it. Here ya go:
ROSES ARE RED
VIOLETS ARE BLUE
I DIG SHOTS AND BEERS
DO YOU LIKE ICE HOCKEY?

ROSE. That's it?

CLIFF. Like it?

ROSE. It's very . . . very interesting.

CLIFF. It's about my mother who was run over by a garbage truck.

ROSE. O. I'm sorry.

CLIFF. What can I say?

ROSE. Did she suffer?

CLIFF. Hey.

ROSE. I'm really sorry.

CLIFF. Me too, being that I pushed her under the wheels. Rose, that's a joke. You know, ha-ha?

ROSE. I don't joke around about that kind of stuff because it was very tragical the way that poor girl kicked the chair out from under herself and then changed her mind.

CLIFF. How do you know that?

ROSE. The police said. And the papers.

CLIFF. How could they know that unless they was here?

ROSE. They said she kicked the chair out from under but changed her mind and reached up for the rope and tried to save herself and they found rope fibers in her palms but her arms got tired and she, you know . . .

CLIFF. She must've been hung up about something.

ROSE. I don't think that's funny.

CLIFF. Well I don't think it's a good subject to make conversation with.

ROSE. Well it's true.

CLIFF. Alotta things are true, but you shouldn't talk about 'em.

ROSE. Why not?

CLIFF. Because no cops and no paper and no poem can give you the bottom line on what's going on in some weirdo's brain when she puts on the rope and leaps into the great ever-after. Even when you got all the facts in your hands, they don't add up to the leap. There's something missing. Maybe she just didn't fit.

She added up the pluses and minuses and figured life ain't worth the hurt. So she turned in her scruples and checked out. And you and the cops and the papers want to know something? She had guts. And I respect that. Alotta people come up with the same figures but they buy insurance. So who knows? Maybe she did the right thing. Maybe she's happy now. Ever think of that?

ROSE. No.

CLIFF. Well you should.

ROSE. I was telling you about the room.

CLIFF. Well I don't want to hear about it.

ROSE. Then drop the subject.

CLIFF. Who brought it up?

ROSE. Me.

CLIFF. Then you drop it. Talk about something nice.

ROSE. Like what?

CLIFF. Like anything.

ROSE. I can't think of something nice.

CLIFF. I can.

ROSE. What?

CLIFF. I can think of something real nice.

ROSE. What?

CLIFF. I can think of something fantastically nice.

ROSE. What?

CLIFF. You.

ROSE. What're you doing?

CLIFF. Taking your poncho.

ROSE. O.

CLIFF. What'd you think?

ROSE. O, I just didn't know why you snuck up on me.

CLIFF. I didn't sneak up.

ROSE. I can take it off.

CLIFF. I know you can.

ROSE. Thank you just the same.

CLIFF. Hang it in the closet?

ROSE. NO!

CLIFF. Sorry.

ROSE. Just lay it on the bed.

CLIFF. How come you whisper?

ROSE. The old lady next door, Mrs. Mancuso. She listens on the wall with a glass.

CLIFF. (*Indicating a spot on the wall.*) Here? (ROSE *shakes her head yes.* CLIFF *punches the wall.*)

ROSE. NO! Don't! She'll hear us!

CLIFF. (*To the wall.*) I don't care if she hears me.

ROSE. I do! She'll tell the landlord and I'll get evicted.

CLIFF. For talking?

ROSE. We're not allowed to have visitors.

CLIFF. How do you know she listens on the walls?

ROSE. I can hear her move the glass.

CLIFF. Beautiful.

CLIFF. How come the window's all boarded up like that?

ROSE. That girl did it. The one who, you know, the rope? My landlord said he would take it down.

CLIFF. Why didn't he?

ROSE. You'll get mad if I tell you.

CLIFF. No I won't.

ROSE. Yes you will.

CLIFF. Why should I get mad?

ROSE. It's not something nice.

CLIFF. C'mon, tell me.

ROSE. You sure?

CLIFF. Yeah.

ROSE. He died.

CLIFF. Don't tell me. Rope?

ROSE. No.

CLIFF. Aspirins?

ROSE. No. He was old.

CLIFF. He died of old age?

ROSE. Yes.

CLIFF. Well, that's alright to die of old age. How old a man was he?

ROSE. O, I don't know. Old.

CLIFF. How old?

ROSE. He was up there.

CLIFF. Give me a rough idea.

ROSE. Over forty.

CLIFF. He must've took good care of himself.

ROSE. I only met him once. He never came around because he couldn't get up stairs so good.

CLIFF. I know. Once you hit forty, stairs are a big problem. So what's the story? You don't have a landlord now?

ROSE. His daughter took over.

CLIFF. So is she gonna take the boards off? Don't tell me! On the way here she was gored by a rhino!

ROSE. No! She said if she hires somebody to take it down, she has to raise the rent, and since I can't afford more rent, I told her leave it up.

CLIFF. I'll take it down.

ROSE. That's alright. I'm used to it.

CLIFF. But you don't have a window. You're missing out on all that wonderful scenery out there.

ROSE. There's nothing but an air shaft.

CLIFF. But you could at least get some fresh air up here.

ROSE. I go for alot of walks.

CLIFF. But you know that smell in this building?

ROSE. I don't smell nothing.

CLIFF. That's mildew.

ROSE. I'm used to it.

CLIFF. It's bad for you. If the window was open it would go away.

ROSE. It's too much trouble.

CLIFF. What trouble? Acouple eight penny nails. I could rip them boards off with bare hands.

ROSE. NO! I'm sorry. It's alright.

CLIFF. I won't hurt your curtains.

ROSE. I'm used to it.

CLIFF. Rose, it's a fire hazard.

ROSE. How can it cause a fire?

CLIFF. It can't cause a fire. But if a fire broke out, how you gonna split?

ROSE. The door.

CLIFF. Suppose the stairs catch fire?

ROSE. They're cement.

CLIFF. It's against the law to board up a window. The landlord has to take it down by law. Not only that, he has to build a fire escape when there's only one means of egress. Not only that, he can't raise the rent because of it. I know the law. Let me take it down in case of fire.

ROSE. What good's that? I'd have to jump five stories.

CLIFF. Hey, would you rather have two broken legs or look like a meatloaf?

ROSE. I don't want to talk about this.

CLIFF. You want to talk about some weirdo who lynched herself but you don't want to talk about saving your life.

ROSE. So you think they're gonna fix your truck today?

CLIFF. Speaking of fire, are they gonna fix your truck. Depends.

ROSE. On what?

CLIFF. Whether the mechanic had a fight with his wife this morning.

ROSE. I don't understand.

CLIFF. Neither do I. And speaking of mechanics, I hate to break the news, but this weed's had it. (*Crumbling a dry, brittle leaf from an obviously dead plant in a flowerpot.*)

ROSE. Nothing grows up here.

CLIFF. No sun.

ROSE. Even the cactus shrivelled up, and they guaranteed it could live anywhere.

CLIFF. Why don't you just throw 'em in the garbage?

ROSE. Well, you never know. They might come alive again.

CLIFF. Come alive again? Never happen.

ROSE. Maybe. I always wanted alot of plants in my room. You know, long ivy vines curling around things and growing up the wall.

CLIFF. Never happen. No sun.

ROSE. You never know. Did you ever hear of Our Lady of Fatima?

CLIFF. Ever hear of Forget About It? No sun, no plants. Now if I took the boards off . . .

ROSE. No sun ever came in the air shaft anyways.

CLIFF. How would you know if the boards were up when you moved in?

ROSE. So what happened to your truck?

CLIFF. Speaking of plants, I dropped reverse gear.

ROSE. Plants?

CLIFF. Gears?

ROSE. Huh?

CLIFF. Reverse?

ROSE. I don't understand.

CLIFF. No reverse, can't back up to the loading dock to unload. Bananas. Very delicate, bananas. Too cold, too hot, or standing too long, they develop a rot inside. Then you can't give 'em away. You even have to pay to dump 'em. And speaking of bananas, want a beer?

ROSE. No.

CLIFF. What's wrong?

ROSE. Nothing.

CLIFF. Mind if I have one?

ROSE. No.

CLIFF. I do something wrong?

ROSE. You drink alot?

CLIFF. What's alot?

ROSE. You get drunk?

CLIFF. Nawwwww.

ROSE. O, good.

CLIFF. Have one with me.

ROSE. No, thank you. I'll have tea.

CLIFF. You don't like beer?

ROSE. One beer wipes me out.

CLIFF. No kidding? C'mon, just one.

ROSE. No, thank you.

CLIFF. It makes you smart.

ROSE. Beer does?

CLIFF. Hey, it made Bud wiser.

ROSE. You like to joke around, huh?

CLIFF. Hey, it's nice to get alittle buzz on now and again. C'mon.

ROSE. Nah.

CLIFF. C'mon, just half.

ROSE. OK. But just half.

CLIFF. And look, if you change your mind about the window, I got a crowbar in my truck.

ROSE. Crowbar?

CLIFF. Yeah.

ROSE. What's that for?

CLIFF. Kill crows.

ROSE. What?

CLIFF. Sure. Alotta people don't realize that in certain remote parts of this country there's what they call the Killer Crow.

ROSE. Never heard of it.

CLIFF. Course not. Washington gave the word to the papers and T.V., play down the Killer Crow. Otherwise you'd have panic in the streets.

ROSE. Really?

CLIFF. Hey, ask any Joe who ever trucked through Arkansas, or worse yet, the Dakota Badlands. Killer Crows as big as doberman pincers with a wing span as wide as this room.

ROSE. Really honest to God?

CLIFF. Hey.

ROSE. Do they attack people?

CLIFF. Attack? Hey, that's all they do. Anything that moves. You don't have to believe me. Go ask the farmers out there. They sit on a cow's head and peck the eyes out.

ROSE. Eughhhhhhh,

CLIFF. That's why they equip us with what they call in the business—a crowbar. When it lands on the hood of the truck and tries to peck your eyes out through the windshield, you grab the crowbar and whack it on the beak—BAM! And it shrieks . . . (*Imitating the crow shriek.*) And flies off.

ROSE. Don't you get ascared?

CLIFF. Hey, I keep a change of underwear in the glove-compartment. But very rarely do you kill one because they got skulls as thick as—pizza crust.

ROSE. Mrs. Mancuso says she sees the landlord's ghost walk through the building the first night of every month.

CLIFF. Here we go.

ROSE. Because he was dead almost two weeks before they found his body and his ghost wandered out his body and that's why they have to bury people right away. Do you think that's true for animals too?

CLIFF. Don't know. It's alittle outside my neighborhood.

ROSE. You believe in ESP?

CLIFF. No, I believe in STP.

ROSE. What's that?

CLIFF. Forget it. Turn on the radio.

ROSE. Don't have one.

CLIFF. What's that? tapes? records?

ROSE. No.

CLIFF. You don't dig music?

ROSE. I hate that music. Hate it. Would you like a glass for your beer?

CLIFF. Hey. Thanks. Where's your glass?

ROSE. I only have one glass.

CLIFF. You entertain much?

ROSE. Beg your pardon?

CLIFF. Forget it. Use the glass.

ROSE. No, you.

CLIFF. (*Putting the glass on her side of the table.*) Now Rose, don't make a big deal. (*Sitting in the chair.*) Sit down. (*Noticing she has no seat.*) What do you do for another chair?

ROSE. The crate. I'll use the crate, you the chair.

CLIFF. No, you the chair, me the crate.

ROSE. No, me the crate, you the chair.

CLIFF. No, you Jane, me Tarzan.

ROSE. You make a joke out of everything, huh?

CLIFF. Hey. (*Pause, to the wall.*) Hey, Mrs. Mafusco, can we borrow your glass?

ROSE. STOP IT!

CLIFF. I was just asking her . . .

ROSE. I'm sorry I ever told you that!

CLIFF. She bugs me that woman.

ROSE. Don't talk then.

CLIFF. She don't bug you?

ROSE. She can't help it. She's on Social Security.

CLIFF. (*Pause. He crinkles the cellophane of his cigarette pack, to wall.*) FIRE!

ROSE. You want me to get evicted?

CLIFF. Naw, I wouldn't want you to lose a place like this.

ROSE. Well?

CLIFF. Well, it's getting late.

ROSE. Guess where I got that chair?

CLIFF. In a chair store.

ROSE. No. C'mon.

CLIFF. Where you work at the Five and Dime.

ROSE. We don't sell chairs. Guess.

CLIFF. Box of crackerjacks?

ROSE. No, cmmon.

CLIFF. Rubbed up against your leg and followed you home.

ROSE. No, c'mon.

CLIFF. The weirdo with the rope left it in her will.

ROSE. That's not funny.

CLIFF. Sorry. Where'd you get it?

ROSE. I don't want to tell you now.

CLIFF. Why not?

ROSE. I just don't. You ruined it all when you said that.

CLIFF. Look, I'm really sorry.

ROSE. Some things aren't funny.

CLIFF. Yeah, I'm gettin the hang of it. So tell me where you got this wonderful chair of yours.

ROSE. No.

CLIFF. Please?

ROSE. Sometimes you joke around too much.

CLIFF. May God strike somebody dead if I should ever do it again. Now c'mon, where'd you get it?

ROSE. I was on my way to the Salvation Army to buy a chair and I saw these people putting garbage on the curb and this old man put this chair on the curb and I asked him if I could have it and he was retired and had diabetes and was cleaning his cellar out and I took the chair home.

CLIFF. Big deal.

ROSE. What?

CLIFF. Big deal.

ROSE. Don't you see? Like it was meant to be.

CLIFF. Meant to be. Hey, tomorrow I'm supposed to see a man about another job. Easier. More bread. More benefits. Closer to home. Dah dah dah dah dah. But my rig broke down and I can't be there, so he'll give the job to somebody else. Now was that meant to be?

ROSE. You can't tell till later.

CLIFF. Hey, c'mon, c'mon, c'mon, meant to be. This morning I'm on the turnpike doin the limit plus to make up for lost time. I get in back of a chicken truck in the passing lane. Big truck with wooden cages tied on the back filled with chickens. That's why they call it a chicken truck. You know, big chickens, little chickens, white chickens, brown chickens, gray chickens. Alotta chickens. And feathers streaming out the back hitting my windshield. Well the driver pulls over so I can pass, but something catches my eye. There's this chicken trying to squeeze between the bars. It has its wings spread full and trying to slip̄ between the bars of the cage. Now I could've passed the chicken truck, but I wanted to see the chicken escape. Don't know why. Just a crazy urge. So I hang back. Sometimes you get so cooped up in the cab you do crazy things. So I start rooting for the chicken. Hey! C'mon! Jump! You chicken punk! Jump!

ROSE. Shhh!

CLIFF. Jump!

ROSE. The old lady!

CLIFF. Hell with the old lady! So I said Jump, baby, jump!

ROSE. Shhhh!

CLIFF. (To wall.) Hey, Rosie, I can't find my underwear.

ROSE. Stop it!

CLIFF. Give the old lady a thrill.

ROSE. That's disgusting.

CLIFF. I was just kidding around.

ROSE. I hate that.

CLIFF. Take it easy.

ROSE. She thinks I'm nice.

CLIFF. I think you're nice too.

ROSE. Well you can go if you want to talk dirty. (*Pause.*) So what happened to the chicken?

CLIFF. The story ends right there.

ROSE. Did it get out?

CLIFF. Yeah.

ROSE. O, good.

CLIFF. Hit the road in front of my wheels. I swerved but it got caught in the back wheels inbetween the double tires. In the rearview all I saw was this feather ball spinning red and white, red and white, feathers spinning off the wheels red and white.

ROSE. (*Pause.*) Did it die?

CLIFF. Very likely with 36,000 pounds rolling over it.

ROSE. Did it suffer?

CLIFF. Nah. Was quick.

ROSE. Did you, you know, go back?

CLIFF. For what?

ROSE. To, you know, pick it up.

CLIFF. No, I left it flat. Pick it up? What am I? a scavenger?

ROSE. No, you know, to bury it.

CLIFF. It was only a chicken.

ROSE. You should of gone back.

CLIFF. Go back shit. I was doin 75 M.P.H. What's amatter?

ROSE. Nothin.

CLIFF. Itchy sweater?

ROSE. Hives.

CLIFF. What from?

ROSE. I just get 'em.

CLIFF. So sudden?

ROSE. YEAH.

CLIFF. Let me scratch.

ROSE. No, it's alright.

CLIFF. Hey, I'm an expert.

ROSE. NO! I'm alright. Thank you just the same.

CLIFF. You scratch like you're tearing off flesh.

ROSE. I hate this.

CLIFF. Maybe you're allergic to wool.

ROSE. It's mohair.

CLIFF. You got mohair than me.

ROSE. It was longer. I just got it cut.

CLIFF. Did your man give you his sweater?

ROSE. What man?

CLIFF. That's a man's sweater you're wearing.

ROSE. No it's not. How do you know? So what if it is?

CLIFF. No big deal.

ROSE. No. Why'd you say that?

CLIFF I was just curious.

ROSE. About what?

CLIFF. Why a girl wears a man's sweater.

ROSE. Alot of girls wear men's sweaters.

CLIFF. You don't have to get so touchy.

ROSE. I'm not touchy.

CLIFF. Alright, drop it.

ROSE. You brought it up.

CLIFF. Well suppose I had on a girl's sweater. Wouldn't you ask why?

ROSE. No. It would be none of my business.

CLIFF. Excuse me. I must be abnormal.

ROSE. Everybody always asks personal questions.

CLIFF. I'm not everybody. I'm Cliff. How ya doin? Nice to meet you. So forget the sweater.

ROSE. Good.

CLIFF. You see, where I come from, men wear men's sweaters and girls . . .

ROSE. I got it from Brenda.

CLIFF. Ahhh, Brenda. Now I understand.

ROSE. I used to live with this girl Brenda.

CLIFF. And was this girl Brenda a man?

ROSE. No. Some guy gave it to her to remember him by.

CLIFF. So why'd she give it to you? Or is that too personal?

ROSE. She didn't give it to me. One night she went down the corner for a pack of cigarettes and never came back no more.

CLIFF. What happened?

ROSE. Nobody knows.

CLIFF. Another mystery. Did you call the police?

ROSB. Of course.

CLIFF. And what'd they say?

ROSE. They put her on the missing persons list.

CLIFF. Good idea. So if she reads the list she'll know she's missing.

ROSE. How she going to see the list if she's missing?

CLIFF. That's the problem. If somebody could find her and give her the list, then she'd know.

ROSE. Know what?

CLIFF. She's missing.

ROSE. I don't think you understand.

CLIFF. Hey, Rose, Rose, Rosie, don't make a big deal. Relax.

ROSE. I can't tell when you kid around because your face is so serious. (*Pause.*) Do you want to have kids?

CLIFF. We got time?

ROSE. Me, I wouldn't want to have kids today, the world being what it is.

CLIFF. What is it?

ROSE. Messed up. Really messed up. I feel sorry for mankind.

CLIFF. Mankind?

ROSE. How it suffers.

CLIFF. Jesus. How come you ask me if I want kids?

ROSE. I don't know. *(Pause.)* Where you from?

CLIFF. Ever hear of Elizabeth?

ROSE. Yeah.

CLIFF. I don't live nowhere near it.

ROSE. C'mon, where?

CLIFF. Trenton.

ROSE. I know Trenton! I went through Trenton once on the train. Trenton has that bridge with that big red neon sign: TRENTON MAKES, THE WORLD TAKES.

CLIFF. They changed it.

ROSE. To what?

CLIFF. WHAT THE WORLD SECRETES, TREN-TON EATS.

ROSE. They did not! I saw this farm from the train window. Just outside Trenton. Someday I want a farm. I want to raise rabbits. Not in cages. Just, you know, free. Running around whe. ver they want. And a little house with red and white curtains and a coop where the rabbits go when it's cold.

CLIFF. Rabbits.

ROSE. They don't have claws, and they can't run that fast, but they zig-zag, and that's what saves them when they're chased.

CLIFF. I bag afew every year in gunning season. They make good stew.

ROSE. I wouldn't sell them for that.

CLIFF. How the hell you gonna make a living? They ain't good for much else except good luck charms to keep keys on.

ROSE. Don't talk about that. Do you ever have dreams like that about a farm or something?

CLIFF. I don't waste my time. I dream of getting from one minute to the next. Beer?

ROSE. Alittle.

CLIFF. So how you gonna latch onto a farm?

ROSE. I don't know.

CLIFF. You think the deed to a farm comes in the morning mail?

ROSE. No.

CLIFF. "Congratulations. You are the happy owner of a sixty acre farm."

ROSE. I don't think that.

CLIFF. You think you could wish it to happen?

ROSE. I was just saying.

CLIFF. It takes scratch, honey. And by the time you earn it you'll forget you ever wanted it. And if you get it, how you gonna make the mortgage payments? the taxes? the upkeep? water, gas, electric? How you gonna feed yourself? And you think it's easy working a farm?

ROSE. No.

CLIFF. It's hard ass-bustin labor and you're in no shape to do it. Rabbits. How you gonna feed 'em?

ROSE. I was just saying. I know I'll never get it. But I can dream if I want.

CLIFF. You can but you can't. It catches up with you. You love something that ain't there and then you start hating what is there, and that's hell.

ROSE. What's your Zodiac sign?

CLIFF. You believe in that crap?

ROSE. It's not . . .

CLIFF. Not what?

ROSE. What you said.

CLIFF. Crap?

ROSE. They proved it's true.

CLIFF. Who proved it?

ROSE. Scientists. When were you born?

CLIFF. Soon after my mother had contractions, and tell you the truth I don't want to hear no bartalk zodiacs with a rising Scorpion on the cusp of diddlydo. Just a bunch of crap some lazyass cooked up to sell a book.

ROSE. You want to go the museum and see a dinosaur? It's about, O, I don't know, fifty or forty feet high. Tyranosaurus.

CLIFF. Do they let you feed it?

ROSE. No! It's dead.

CLIFF. Rope!

ROSE. No! It's all bones. Bones this thick all wired together. I made friends with the curator and he took me in the cellar and showed me how they wire the bones.

CLIFF. In the cellar, eh?

ROSE. Of the museum.

CLIFF. And did he show you his bone?

ROSE. No. The bones belong to the museum.

CLIFF. O, I see.

ROSE. He told me the dinosaurs disappeared off the face of the earth very suddenly.

CLIFF. How come?

ROSE. Nobody knows.

CLIFF. Mysterious.

ROSE. They think it was the temperature.

CLIFF. They died of fever?

ROSE. No. The climate changed and the dinosaurs couldn't get used to it. It was called The Great Ice Age.

CLIFF. Why didn't they go to Florida?

ROSE. You want to hear this? This is a serious subject.

CLIFF. I know. Never know when you might come across a dinosaur.

Rose. And guess what? They just found a wooly mammoth in Siberia, or Algeria, or, I don't know, someplace far. And it was froze in ice in perfect condition! like it was in a refrigerator for ten thousand years! C'mon. We still have a chance before the museum closes.

Cliff. That's romantic as hell. Go look at bones.

Rose. People who can't appreciate culture are just ignorant.

Cliff. I must be people.

Rose. Mankind does not understand its past.

Cliff. That what the museum guy says? Tell him if he wants to know about mankind, tell him stop playing with his bone down in the cellar there and go in a city where you don't know anybody and have your truck breakdown and try and get somebody give you a hand! Don't tell me about bones.

Rose. It's interesting.

Cliff. Yeah, so are rock fights. Look, Rose, I'm not too big on culture, see. Now I can get all hepped up over a t-bone or prime rib, but that's about it for bones.

Rose. I don't think you understand.

Cliff. Hey, look, sweetheart, I understand. I got a few hours to kill in Philly and I'm not gonna spend it looking at bones. Hey, why don't we hoof it to a joint, lay out some frogskin, do a pizza with the works to go, jump on some vino, bring it here, chow down, talk about the moon, a couple laughs, sing, dance, waterski, la la la, whatever.

Rose. I have food here.

Cliff. I don't want to use your food.

Rose. I have a lot of food.

Cliff. C'mon, what do you want to do—it's up to me.

Rose. I'd rather stay here.

Cliff. Terrific. What do you got?

ROSE. This.

CLIFF. Boneless sardines.

ROSE. Magic mountain herb tea. And this.

CLIFF. Cranberry sauce. Dusseldorff mustard.

ROSE. Bouillon cubes. Cinnamon sticks. And this!

CLIFF. My favorite! Sea-weed soup!

ROSE. I got that in a health store.

CLIFF. I thought maybe a pet shop.

ROSE. Dried fruits and nuts. Corn niblets. Artichokes hearts. Asparagus. Jerkins.

CLIFF. Jerkins? (*Opening the refrigerator, coming up with a limp celery stalk.* ROSE *grabs it out of his hand and tosses it in the garbage.*) Hey! Don't!

ROSE. It's wilted.

CLIFF. (*Picking it out of the garbage.*) Never know. It might come alive again. (ROSE *throws it back in the garbage.*) You live on this stuff?

ROSE. I get fruits and vegetables on Ninth Street when they close.

CLIFF. What, steal it?

ROSE. No, you should see the good stuff they throw away.

CLIFF. Garbage?

ROSE. I wash it off. They throw away lettuce leaves just because it has a brown edge. Or if a peach has a bruise, I cut it out. And stick bread this long. A day old. But I don't eat it all. I break it up and feed the pigeons on the roof.

CLIFF. Get your poncho. I'll take you out for a steak.

ROSE. I thought you wanted to make something here?

CLIFF. Out of this shit? I'd have to be a goddamn magician.

ROSE. You don't have to curse.

CLIFF. What'd I say?

ROSE. You cursed.

CLIFF. No shit.

ROSE. If you want to curse, you can do it somewheres else.

CLIFF. You don't curse?

ROSE. No.

CLIFF. Bull shit.

ROSE. I don't. And don't say I do.

CLIFF. You never cursed?

ROSE. Never. Not once.

CLIFF. No shit? Why not?

ROSE. Because.

CLIFF. Why because?

ROSE. Because I don't. That's all.

CLIFF. What do you say when you stub your toe? O chocolate kisses?

ROSE. I say ouch. And I don't like people who curse.

CLIFF. So you don't like me.

ROSE. Not when you curse like that.

CLIFF. So what are you, a nun?

ROSE. No.

CLIFF. Eh, Sister Rose?

ROSE. If you don't like it ...

CLIFF. Stick it?

ROSE. No.

CLIFF. Sit on it?

ROSE. No!

CLIFF. Shove it?

ROSE. No!

CLIFF. Fry it up with onions? what? if I don't like it what? Eh, Sister Rose?

ROSE. If you don't like it you can go.

CLIFF. For cursing?

ROSE. Yes.

CLIFF. Why?

Rose. It's ugly.

Cliff. I didn't invent it.

Rose. You use it.

Cliff. It's part of the language.

Rose. Not my language.

Cliff. Hey, sorry. I meant to say all shucks and golly gee.

Rose. Don't make fun of me.

Cliff. I'm not.

Rose. I hate when they make fun of me.

Cliff. You make a big deal out of every fuckin thing.

Rose. STOP IT! I hate that!

Cliff. I'm sorry.

Rose. No you're not! I hate when they curse. Like them kids at the zoo. I hate it.

Cliff. Here we go.

Rose. Their radios up against their ears and that wild ugly music and cursing! I hate that!

Cliff. What kids?

Rose. I hate that.

Cliff. What kids at the zoo?

Rose. Nothing.

Cliff. They cursed at you?

Rose. No. At those birds.

Cliff. O, they cursed at those birds, eh?

Rose. I forget their names.

Cliff. O, so you're on a first-name basis with those birds, eh, Rose?

Rose. Those tall birds with the long thin legs.

Cliff. Ah, yes. The tall thin-legged bird of North America.

Rose. Derricks!

Cliff. Derricks?

Rose. No. Cranes. Some kind of cranes.

CLIFF. And what did the derricks say, Rose?

ROSE. Stop making fun of me.

CLIFF. Did the derricks ask you if you needed a lift?

ROSE. You may think it's funny but I was the last one to see them alive last summer. There was only seven of them in the world and the zoo had four of them. I used to walk there every night just to watch them stand so still in the water. And they walked so graceful, in slow motion. And they have legs as skinny as my little finger. Long legs. And there was only seven in the world because they killed them off for feathers for ladies hats or something. And one night a gang of boys came by with radios to their ears and cursing real bad, you know, F, and everything. And I was, you know, ascared. And they started saying things to me, you know, dirty things, and laughing at the birds. And one kid threw a stone to see how close he could splash the birds, and then another kid tried to see how close he could splash the birds, and then they all started throwing stones to splash the birds, and then they started throwing stones *at the* birds, and I started screaming STOP IT! and a stone hit a bird's leg and it bended like a straw and the birds keeled over in the water, flapping wings in the water, and the kids kept laughing and throwing stones and I kept screaming STOP IT! STOP IT! but they couldn't hear me through that ugly music on the radios and kept laughing and cursing and throwing stones, and I ran and got the zoo guard and he got his club and we ran to the place of the birds but the kids were gone. And there was white feathers on the water. And the water was real still. And there was big swirls of blood. And the birds were real still. Their beaks alittle open. Legs broke. Toes curled. Still. Like the world stopped. And the guard said something to me but I couldn't hear him. I just saw his mouth moving. And I started screaming. And the cops came and took me the hospital and they gave me a needle to make me stop screaming. And they never caught the gang. But even if they did, what good's that? They can't make the birds come alive again.

CLIFF. (*Long pause.*) Yeah, well. I'm really sorry to hear about it. But the fact of the matter is . . . it's a rough-tough world out there, and like everything else, if the birds can't hack the jive, maybe it's better they're not around gettin in the way because if you want to survive you got to be rough and tough right back.

ROSE. But they don't have a way to be rough and tough.

CLIFF. Then maybe it was meant to be for 'em to bite the dust.

ROSE. That's mean.

CLIFF. That's life.

ROSE. That's not life.

CLIFF. That's the way Niagra Falls.

ROSE. You're just as bad as them.

CLIFF. I'm not them. I'm me.

ROSE. You stick up for them, you mise well be them!

CLIFF. Hey, did I kill the birds? Did I?

ROSE. You mise well if you stick up for them!

CLIFF. But did I kill the fuckin birds?

ROSE. NO! (*Pause. Apologetic for screaming.*) No. (*Pause.*) I think you should go.

CLIFF. Yeah, me too. Afterall, you don't want it to get around you hang out with bird killers. Well, kid, it was nice.

ROSE. You think they fixed your truck?

CLIFF. No. Wasn't meant to be.

ROSE. I hope you get the new job.

CLIFF. As they say when you can't stop your rig— them's the breaks.

ROSE. What kind of job is it?

CLIFF. Testing parachutes.

ROSE. What kind of job is that?

CLIFF. Fifty bucks an hour plus they let you keep the chutes that don't open.

ROSE. What would you do with a parachute?

CLIFF. Make handkerchiefs. Big ones. (*Pause. They face each other.* CLIFF *offers a handshake. She slowly accepts.*) Cold hands.

ROSE. I'm anemic.

CLIFF. Know what's good for that?

ROSE. What?

CLIFF. Boneless sardines. Hey, Rosie-posey, mind if I smoke?

ROSE. No, but don't call me that.

CLIFF. Why not?

ROSE. You're making fun.

CLIFF. No I'm not. Honest. I just can't believe somebody like you exists.

ROSE. What do you mean somebody like me?

CLIFF. I mean you're beautiful.

ROSE. Don't say that kind of stuff to me. I know I'm not beautiful. You're making fun.

CLIFF. I'm afraid to talk. Everything I say hurts you. Maybe I don't use the right words. Hey, I'm gonna watch myself from now on. Wanna do some stuff?

ROSE. Beg your pardon?

CLIFF. You dig the weed?

ROSE. What weed?

CLIFF. C'mon, you're joshin me now.

ROSE. I don't understand.

CLIFF. Wanna do a joint?

ROSE. I don't understand.

CLIFF. Would you like a cigarette?

ROSE. I don't smoke, thank you. What's that?

CLIFF. Paper.

ROSE. What for?

CLIFF. Make cigarettes.

ROSE. Like the cowboys?

CLIFF. Yeah, the cowboys. Ride 'em cowboy. Hey.

ROSE. What?

CLIFF. Yippi hi ho kai yea!

ROSE. I don't see why you don't just buy 'em out a machine like everybody else.

CLIFF. I may have to. My grocer went on vacation for three to five years.

ROSE. Isn't that a long time for vacation?

CLIFF. That's what he told the judge.

ROSE. Eughhhhhhhh.

CLIFF. Eh?

ROSE. Smells.

CLIFF. Do a drag.

ROSE. No. It's awful. What's that?

CLIFF. Roach clip.

ROSE. What's that for?

CLIFF. Kill roaches. You grab 'em by the antenna and twist. Screws up their radar and they start walkin crooked and bump into things and die of multiple bruises.

ROSE. Get out!

CLIFF. Take a toke.

ROSE. No thank you.

CLIFF. It makes the world go bye-bye.

ROSE. What do you mean?

CLIFF. I mean I want to hold you, Rosie Rosie.

ROSE. So why do you want to change jobs?

CLIFF. Do you scrub yourself with a wire brush? You are so immaculate.

ROSE. So it's a better job?

CLIFF. How's a man supposed to get near you, Rosie?

ROSE. I think I'd like to be a trucker--I mean, you know, if I was a man.

CLIFF. If I was me, I'd want to be a refrigerator. What problems can a refrigerator have? OK, alittle defrosting every six months. Big deal. Ok, afew mouldy cucumber and slimy heads of lettuce to throw away. But outside of that, what? So what am I sayin? A wish's just a detour. Skip it.

ROSE. How come you make that noise?

CLIFF. To get all the vitamins out.

ROSE. You don't make sense. *(CLIFF goes to wash off dirt from the beer can.)* Hot is cold and cold is hot.

CLIFF. Yeah, I got one something like that, except on mine, hot is cold and cold is also cold.

ROSE. What's your place like?

CLIFF. A floor that leads to walls that lead to a roof that mostly keeps off the rain. And dust that looks like furniture.

ROSE. You don't dust?

CLIFF. Never home.

ROSE. Why even have an apartment?

CLIFF. I need an address.

ROSE. What for?

CLIFF. So people could send me bills.

ROSE. Bills for what?

CLIFF. For the rent and the phone and the electricity and the heat I never use.

ROSE. That's crazy.

CLIFF. Hey.

ROSE. What?

CLIFF. Touch me.

ROSE. What for?

CLIFF. I'm not sure you're really there.

ROSE. You're silly.

CLIFF. You remind me of somebody I never knew.

ROSE. I hate that noise. Don't you hate people who make noise when they eat soup?

CLIFF. Only if it's my soup.

ROSE. It must be nice to be a trucker.

CLIFF. Beautiful.

ROSE. Different restaurents everyday...

CLIFF. Sunnyside ulcers with a side of ptomaine...

ROSE. Always moving...

CLIFF. Always a stranger...

CLIFF. Hitchhikers. Every other one, Charles Manson, the ones in between, some runaway moonie...

ROSE. Ocean to ocean...

CLIFF. Roads that lead to highways that go on forever...

Rose. I never saw the ocean.

Cliff. Never?

Rose. Nope.

Cliff. Where you been all your life?

Rose. What's it like?

Cliff. The ocean?

Rose. Yeah.

Cliff. *(Making an expansive gesture. Pause.)* Alotta water.

Rose. Big?

Cliff. Pshew.

Rose. Really?

Cliff. Hey, like the sky, but down here.

Rose. Unhuh ...

Cliff. Blue water, white water...

Rose. Unhuh ...

Cliff. Seagulls flying low over the water... *(Imitating the cry of the gull.)*

Rose. Is that how they sound?

Cliff. No, that's me when I'm stuck in a hot truck. You come down a mountain and see them heat waves rollin off that asphalt, and then you see all that cool clean water out there, and you'd like to pull off the road and run across that beach and let them foamy waves take you under. But you can't.

Rose. Sharks.

Cliff. No. You got deadlines. You got schedules.

Rose. But at least you see the ocean.

Cliff. Just enough to tease.

Rose. It must be wonderful.

Cliff. Beautiful.

Rose. Free as a bird.

Cliff. Free. What's free? Pushin an eight year old played-out dog on retreads that drops a gearbox when you get alittle ahead of schedule? Free. You say free cause you're stuck behind a candy counter all day and a Five and Dime don't move. Free. When a dispatcher slips you an extra yard to overload your rig, you ain't free to turn it down, because it's your bread and butter. Without the butter. So now you got to sneak past the scale stations where these jerky little guys with clipboards and 27 pens in their shirt pocket wait for you and your freedom to come 18-wheelin down Primrose Pike. Flags you over. Weighs the rig. You get a fine that wipes out the bribe you just took. Click a button and you got a thousand good buddies who map you a snakepath on backroads that never heard of rules and regulations. But then, out of nowhere, a little yellow flasher comes up in the rearview. Motor Vehicle Inspector out looking for his afternoon quota. Pulls you over. You know he's gonna weigh the rig and slap another summons on you. You know he's gonna crank up his portable scales. Gets out his car like John Wayne with an A-bomb in his holster. Sunglasses so you can't see his eyes. Asks for your logbook, please. Always says please. Looks at it. Scans your eyes that look more like roadmaps than roadmaps. Closes it. Hands it back. Knows it's all faked up. Knows you wrote "rest" every 450 miles even when you took no rest because that's the law. But he can't prove it. So to show his boss he wasn't strokin the breeze, he gets you for something else. Dead tail light. Missing mud flap. Dirty license plate. He's a bonafide specialist in smallness.

"Take a seat in the back of the car, please."
"Hey, look, buddy, could you give me a break?"

He pretends he don't hear. And you got to sit there and listen to his pen skip. And trucks are passing you. Trucks with no tail lights. Trucks with no mud flaps. Trucks with bond papers expired. Trucks with last year's license plates. But he's got you. And you sit there. And you think. You think of the money. You think of the doctor who said rattling around in that bucket of clankity junk's giving you the bladder of a 75 year old. You think of your woman. Wonder what she's doing. And who she's doing it with. For a second you don't blame her. Then he hands you the summons. Puts you in the hole half a yard. Gun the engine. Pop a benzedrine. Hit the road. You never turn around. Never. Tires up on the curb on a narrow street in Baltimore. Stacking the load on the curb. A rusty old man who's been cheating death for 10 years comes running out the store waving his arms.

"Hey, buddy, could you bring it in that door for me?"
"Sorry, pal. Bill of lading says sidewalk delivery."
"But can't you just wheel it in for me, buddy. Take you two seconds."
"I do what the order says, pal."

You really want to help the guy, but why should you? Hey, sometimes you're the bird, and sometimes you're the windshield. Today, you get to be the bird.

"Sorry, pal. I go by the bill."

And he slips you a sawbuck. Stuff it in your shirt. And you say:

"Where would you like it, sir?"

Score's even. Next stop, the docks. Pull in. Dispatcher stands there pencil and clipboard checking off unicorns. Pretends he don't see you. You snap on your smile:

"Hey, how ya doin, champ?"
"What can I do for you?"
"Look, buddy, I'm running a little late and I got to blow this town in an hour."
"You got an appointment?"
"Appointment? What're you? a frickin dentist? Why can't I pull in that spot and unload?"
"No room."
"No room? What's that empty space there?"
"That docks reserved. You got to wait."
"How long?"
"Till there's room."
"How long's that about?"
"You tell me."

Here's another punk you want to bust in the snotbox. But, hey, you asked to get in the game, so play by the rules. You hand him the sawbuck the old man slipped you. And you get alittlc surprise. He hands it back and walks away. Slow. Now you want to rip his arm off and slap him across the face with it. But that ain't in Murphy's Law: You can't quit, you can't win, you can't break even. So you peel off a double saw. He takes it like he grabbed an ass. Like it never happened. Says like an old beer buddy:

"Back it in, Amigo. Have you truckin in a snap."

You swear this is your last run. Breeze through the want ads. You're not ACCOUNTANT. DISHWASHER AND GRAVEDIGGER don't appeal. Only thing you're really qualified for is PLASMA DONOR URGENTLY NEEDED. Next thing you know, you're upshifting through an amber light. And not to hear a personal question you're about to ask, you turn up the radio. But they don't play the good songs no more. They just play them new songs. "O baby o baby o baby o baby I want you o baby I need you o baby drop your laundry." They got shoemakers makin songs. Fidgit on the CB. Talk ice patches. Radar traps. See a phone booth. Choke it with quarters, dimes, nickles. She's not there. Do a hundred miles. Blinking neon. Diner. Pull over. Coffee, danish, small talk. Do your little routine. Make a waitress laugh. Find out Johnny Blade fell asleep at the wheel out Nevada. Through a guardrail. 200 feet. Now he's truckin in a wheelchair. Do a hundred miles. You think of that waitress in the last diner and sleep. And if you had a choice, you'd take sleep. But you don't. Drink black coffee till you can't taste nothin' but the hotness. You get used to your own stink. No bath, three days. Phone booth. Let it ring thirty times. She's not there. **Four in the goddamn morning. Not home. You start** talkin to yourself. You argue with yourself. Whether she this, me that. Whether you should pull over and sleep or do another hundred miles. You argue, you lose, you win, you doze. Rig edges into the other lane. Guy in a Volkswagon beeps like crazy. You see his mouth moving behind the windshield. He's in the right, but you curse him, his family, his car, dog, kids that ain't born yet. Pull over. Lay on the front seat. Tell yourself you're just resting your eyes because the load's got to be in San Jose in 6 hours or they don't want it, and by rough calculations you can't make it in less than seven and a half. Lay your arm over your face to block out the sun. You see the veins in your wrist, red and blue, like roads on the map. And that question you been giving the slips for the last thousand miles catches up, and you whisper to nobody in particular, "What am I doing? What am I doing?" And you fade. Wonderful. It scares you. You spring up. You think you slept 10 hours. It's only 2 minutes. The Volkswagon passing you. Other trucks passing you. Leap to the wheel. Pop a benny. Peel off. Insect hits the windshield. Leaves its soft green smear ontop a thousand others. Count the white lines shooting past. Lose count. Lose touch. Lose yourself in the road. And you're caught. You move with the pack. Keep it between the lines. That's what it comes down to. Keep it movin even though the road funnels into some gigantic meatgrinder and every robot's over the limit to be the first one inside where it's all mangled and mixed and you holler, SLOW DOWN! but they only see your mouth movin behind the windshield. Bulldog tailgating, poundin foghorn to make you go faster into the grinder. Sign reads NO STOPPING OR STANDING. Radio's goin "O baby o baby." Three lanes merge into two. The broken white line becomes a solid yellow line, and the solid fades and two lanes merge into one. You floor it. Into the tunnel. Engine echoes off the walls, drowns out your brain.

Air goes rancid. Roll up the window. Radio goes dead. Turn on the lights. Lights dim out. Flying down into the tunnel. You look for a miracle. You see a diner ahead. You notice your right blinker clicking.

ROSE. *(Long pause.)* You're right. Get the parachute job. *(Pause.)* The furtherest I ever been was Newark, New Jersey.

CLIFF. Beautiful.

ROSE. I saved up to see the Statue of Liberty, and I asked the ticket man for a ticket to New York, and he thought I said *Newark,* and I spent the whole day there, in the train station.

CLIFF. Someday I'm gonna take you cross country in my truck.

ROSE. Are you joking now?

CLIFF. Hey.

ROSE. Do they allow that?

CLIFF. It's my truck. I'll let you hold the crowbar.

ROSE. Get out.

CLIFF. Hey, just when you think you had it, you come around a mountain and the Pacific Ocean kicks you right in the eyeballs.

Rose. People always promise things, but they don't really mean it.

Cliff. Hey, once more: I'm not people. I'm me. And speaking of nothing in particular, you got a beautiful mouth, but the only thing I don't like about it is I'm not close enough. *(He kisses her with a kind of sublimated violence, but breaks gently. Pause.)*

Rose. Thank you.

Cliff. You don't have to say thank you when a man kisses you.

Rose. Do you have to make fun of everything I do?

Cliff. Hey.

Rose. What?

Cliff. You like me?

Rose. Yes.

Cliff. I don't blame you. I'm a hellava guy. Hey, I need to hold you.

Rose. What for?

Cliff. I don't get much exercise.

Rose. Everybody wants to touch and say nice things.

Cliff. Hey, it's normal.

ROSE. And then you never see them no more.

CLIFF. It's natural.

ROSE. Says who?

CLIFF. The world.

ROSE. If it's natural, what am I?

CLIFF. You tell me.

ROSE. A freak?

CLIFF. You said it, not me.

ROSE. Alright, so I'm a freak.

CLIFF. I need to hold you. Can't you see that?

ROSE. I'd rather be a freak than end up like Brenda.

CLIFF. Here we go.

ROSE. Some guy stopped his car when she was walking down the street. He had a beautiful white car with furry seats. And he said all these things. Took her for a ride, saying all these things, you know, nice things. And they drank this wine— (*Showing her Mateus bottle.*) which costs, for your information, $179.00 a bottle! And he said these things and she, you know, got crazy for him. And the night was beautiful. And he said he'd come by the next day but he didn't, so she went to his apartment and his car was there and she knocked on the door but he wouldn't answer because he had another girl in there. And Brenda kicked the door, and he still wouldn't open it, and she got sick and vomited on his porch and let herself fall in the snow. In the snow. And she felt the snow freezing her fingers and toes, and she didn't care what happened anymore, and the cops came in the morning and found her almost dead and dragged her in their car and took her the hospital and she almost got killed of pneumonia and frost-bite and they gave her a needle to make her stop screaming and put her the eighth floor and psychiatrists asked Brenda why she did it, lay in the snow, and she told them and they didn't believe her and they found her father but he didn't want her and used to beat her and curse at her and other stuff and he was an alcoholic and they kept her up there two months and she lost her job and they . . . And that's what happened to Brenda.

CLIFF. So what.

ROSE. What do you mean so what?

CLIFF. That's English for so what.

ROSE. So that's true love.

CLIFF. O don't make me barff. She was a true asshole.

ROSE. When you love somebody, you don't curse or make fun and even when they cheat you make a fool of yourself even if you have to sit in the snow and die.

CLIFF. O, cut the shit, huh? There's no such thing as true love. True love's when you got a fat bankbook.

ROSE. Maybe for some people.

CLIFF. Hey, one thing counts out there, Rosie-schmosie. Scratch! And you gotta leap in the fuckin dogfight and grab all you can grab. And while you're out grabbin it, true love's screwin the guy next door. And if you lose it, you get true love's consolation prize —alimony payments! So don't hit me with this stale bag of wholesale pigshit about true love because I been there and I know better. (*Pause.*) Alls I said was I want to hold you and you gotta make a big deal.

ROSE. It's not my fault I'm this way!

CLIFF. Look, I don't want to hear about no bad childhood.

ROSE. I have to be very careful because of my hemophilia.

CLIFF. Your what?

ROSE. I happen to have a very very rare blood disease. If I get cut I could bleed to death.

CLIFF. This ain't happening.

ROSE. Just alittle scratch bleeds for days! And if I get a deep cut, that's it!

CLIFF. I said I want to hold you, not bite you!

ROSE. So I have to be very careful!

CLIFF. So how's a flesh and blood man supposed to get near you? I talk, I draw blood. I touch, you go icy. I mean, hey, maybe we should carry this thing on over the telephone. Germless. And when it starts to hurt, you could hang up.

ROSE. I don't have a phone.

CLIFF. I'm not talking about phones! I'm talking about me and you! I'm here, you're there, and there's no wall between us except the one you keep building up in that head of yours!

ROSE. I don't know what wall you're talking about.

CLIFF. Hey, Rosie, I didn't order a pound of non-pariels because I got a sweettooth. I didn't come up here to discuss Brenda or seaweed soup or homophillioes or dinosaurs or flamingoes. I came up here to be with you. You. And hold you. Make love to you.

ROSE. (*Pause.*) I don't want to cheat.

CLIFF. So you do have a man, eh?

ROSE. Yes.

CLIFF. So why the fuck did you invite me up here.

ROSE. And he doesn't curse or smoke or pretend he wants to talk when he wants to touch and doesn't make fun!

CLIFF. What's he, a priest? Sister Rose and Father Clean!

ROSE. Shut up!

CLIFF. What do you guys do for thrills? whip each other with the rosaries?

ROSE. Be quiet.

CLIFF. Hallujah! Father Clean and the Boneless Sardine!

ROSE. I hate you!

CLIFF. O gosh! I think I'll go hang myself!

ROSE. You're just like them!

CLIFF. I think I'll go the zoo and stone a long-legged derrick!

ROSE. Stop it!

CLIFF. Or jump out the window! But how can I? Some whacko boarded it up and another whacko won't take it down!

ROSE. Go to hell!

CLIFF. You cursed! O, what a trashmouth! Mrs. Majusko! Call the Sanitation Department!

ROSE. FUCK YOU!

CLIFF. Rose, you don't watch your mouth, I'm leavin.

ROSE. Now for the rest of my life, I could never say I never cursed!

CLIFF. O big fuckin deal! That your only problem in life? You been cooped up too long, Rosie-dozie!

ROSE. If I never met you, this would've never happened!

CLIFF. If! If! If! If my aunt had balls, she'd be my uncle! (*Pause.*) Well, look, champ, I was lookin for alittle wham-bam-thank-you-m'am, but I guess I turned over the wrong rock. So, catch ya later.

ROSE. Can I have your sweater?

CLIFF. Come again?

ROSE. Nevermind.

CLIFF. No no no no no. What did you ask me?

ROSE. Nothing . . . I was just . . . Nothing.

CLIFF. Could you have my sweater?

ROSE. If you don't want it.

CLIFF. Well, yeah, I was just about to toss it in the garbage on the way out.

ROSE. You must think I'm crazy.

CLIFF. Noooooooooooooooooo000.

ROSE. Nevermind.

CLIFF. Can I ask what for?

ROSE. I don't know. To remember you by.

CLIFF. Remember me by.

ROSE. But nevermind.

CLIFF. It's my work sweater.

ROSE. I should've never asked.

CLIFF. It's dirty and I slept in it. Blew my nose in it.

ROSE. Nevermind.

CLIFF. You don't want me to stay but you want to remember me by. That's one that goes way over my head, champ. So let's just leave it at that. Take good care of it. It's used to travelling across country at 65 m.p.h.

ROSE. Thank you.

CLIFF. And be careful. It goes through amber lights.

ROSE. Thank you.

CLIFF. It's 100% virgin wool. Meant to be. For you.

ROSE. Thank you.

CLIFF. The label fell out. But see this hole?

ROSE. Yes?

CLIFF. I burned it there so I know which's the front. But I don't want to assume anything, Rosie. Maybe you like the front on the back. Me myself, I like the front on the front.

ROSE. Thank you.

CLIFF. Rose?

ROSE. Yeah?

CLIFF. Can I have your shoe?

ROSE. I thought you was different.

CLIFF. It was all in your head. Catch ya later.

ROSE. Bye.

CLIFF. Yeah.

ROSE. Hope you get the new job.

CLIFF. Yeah.

ROSE. Think your truck's fixed?

CLIFF. What's it matter?

ROSE. Will you ever drive through Philadelphia again?

CLIFF. Who knows?

ROSE. Bye.

CLIFF. Yeah.

ROSE. Thank you.

CLIFF. Yeah.

ROSE. Bye. Cliff?

CLIFF. Yeah?

ROSE. Will you be cold without your sweater?

CLIFF. Me? Cold? Hey, Rosie, you're lookin at the only survivor of the Great Ice Age. (*Exit* CLIFF. *His footfalls fade down the stairwell.* ROSE *rushes to the door.*)

ROSE. Cliff? (*Lights fade quickly.*)

### *END OF ACT ONE*

## ACT TWO

*The same. Almost complete darkness.* ROSE *hardly visible in bed.*

ROSE. Shhh! The old lady! Hear her move the glass? (*Pause.*) You have cold feet. You should cut your toe-nails. (*Pause.*) If your truck ever crashes through a guardrail off a mountain, and you get all crippled up in a wheelchair, don't worry. Everything will still be the same. (*Pause.*) And I don't cheat. Shh! Hear her move the glass? She's hard-of-hearing until you whisper. And then she hears the flowers growing on the wallpaper. Around Christmas she goes a little berzerk. Screams at her son for not visiting her. Throws things. Pots and dishes. But he's not there. Nobody's there. And then it gets real quiet, and if you listen close, like with a glass, you can hear her whimper, like a hurt animal. (*Pause.*) You should rub your hands with coldcreme to make 'em soft. You scratch me. (*Pause.*) When you was asleep, I dreamed we were in your truck, riding up this mountain, you know, cross country. (*Pause.*) If you don't mean something, don't tell me, alright? Because it makes me dream, and one dream makes another, and I'm lost in the bigness of the mountain and the curve of the road, and the engine was chugging hard, and there was this thin guardrail this far away and the breeze carried the scent of grass and wild flowers and I got ascared because we got higher and higher and held tight to the seat and you laughed and said, "what's that funny noise?" and I said, "what noise?" and you said, "o no! the truck's gonna explode!" and I punched you and we laughed and this cool breeze, this different breeze

**46**

touched us, this salt breeze, and we came around the bend in the mountain road and all of a sudden this tremendous bright light hit us, and it was so big you couldn't see the beginning or the end and it was the Pacific Ocean glimmering like tin foil rolled out forever, and we couldn't speak for a long time, and way down below us we saw the cities along the coast, like beads on a necklace, and we went down the mountain. And at the bottom we got out the truck and you took my arm and pulled me across the sand and into the waves and I screamed at the touch of the water and you laughed and we both went under and tasted the salt of the ocean and it was so good and we came up and kissed me hard on the mouth and I tasted your salt and a wave came over our heads and dunked us under and we laughed and got water in our mouths and spit it at each other and everybody on the beach thought we was crazy but we didn't care because we felt new again. (*A knock at the door.*)

CLIFF. Rose?

ROSE. Yes?

CLIFF. It's me.

ROSE. Yes?

CLIFF. Cliff.

ROSE. Yes?

CLIFF. I want to see you. (*Pause.*) Rose? (*Pause.*) Can I see you? (*Pause.*) Huh? Rose?

ROSE. Yes?

CLIFF. You alone? (*Pause.*) Rose?

ROSE. Yes?

CLIFF. You alone?

ROSE. Yes.

CLIFF. You sure?

ROSE. I know if I'm alone or not!

CLIFF. Can I see you?

ROSE. What for?

CLIFF. I don't know I don't know I don't know.
(*Pause.*) Can I?

ROSE. I have to get up early for work.

CLIFF. Me too, but I have to see you tonight, Rose.

ROSE. What for? slam-bam and thank you ma'm?

CLIFF. Hey, Rose . . .

ROSE. Well I'm not a slam-bam!

CLIFF. That was just all mouth . . .

ROSE. There's alot of slam-bams in the world!

CLIFF. I know, I know . . .

ROSE. But I am not a slam-bam!

CLIFF. I never thought you was . . .

ROSE. You said you came here for slam-bam.

CLIFF. Rose, can we talk?

ROSE. I don't want to hear about your waitresses or
your frickin truck. (*Pause.*) You there? (*Pause.*) Cliff?
(*She opens the door. The door stops with a jerk when
the chain runs out. Through the long space, a rude
slice of hallway light glares on* ROSE *and* CLIFF.)

CLIFF. Hey, Rosie, you're wearin my sweater.

ROSE. Truck break down again?

CLIFF. Not the truck.

ROSE. I thought you never go back.

CLIFF. Yeah, me too. Can I come in?

ROSE. No.

CLIFF. What?

ROSE. No.

CLIFF. That's what I thought you said. Rose?

ROSE. What?

CLIFF. You don't open up and I pee in the hallway
and you get evicted.

ROSE. (*She tries to close the door but for* CLIFF's
*foot.*) Goodbye.

CLIFF. Have a good life.

ROSE. It's over.

CLIFF. Over? Where was I?

ROSE. Get your foot out please?

CLIFF. Did I enjoy it?

ROSE. Your foot, please!

CLIFF. If it ever gets started again, let me know, eh?

ROSE. Goodbye. (*She slams the door, listens to the silence, pause.*) I know you're there.

CLIFF. No sir.

ROSE. Will you please leave?

CLIFF. Alright, but before I leave, I have one last and final thing to say to your face.

ROSE. (*Opening the door.*) What?

CLIFF. I'm not leaving.

ROSE. I wish I never met you.

CLIFF. That's why you wear my sweater.

ROSE. So.

CLIFF. So.

ROSE. So what?

CLIFF. To remember me by.

ROSE. I thought you had deadlines and schedules.

CLIFF. Remember what about me?

ROSE. It's all ruined now, so nevermind.

CLIFF. Remember what?

ROSE. You won't understand.

CLIFF. Try me. In school, you know, I was the fastest one in the slow group.

ROSE. It's personal.

CLIFF. So's my sweater.

ROSE. You want it back?

CLIFF. Remember what about me?

ROSE. That look you had in the Five and Dime.

CLIFF. What look?

ROSE. That look when you came up to my, you know, candy counter. When I was cleaning the glass, dreaming a man would come in that door out of the cold, with a smile you could hang onto, and he would notice me and we could talk without words. And the door opened and you walked in, came up to my counter and pressed your greasy finger on the glass and said, "Hey, sweetheart, gimme a pound of them things, nonpariels," and I looked at your fingerprint, and you did a beautiful thing: wiped it off with your sweater sleeve.

CLIFF. I did? O yeah, sure.

ROSE. And nobody does that. Nobody. And I got ascared, you know, that I could make a thing come true, and you started to walk away and I made a dream you'd stay and you turned around with this look . . . But all it said was, she's a slam-bam!

CLIFF. How do you know?

ROSE. She's a cooped-up whacko!

CLIFF. Rose . . .

ROSE. That's all it said.

CLIFF. Maybe I'm a cooped-up whacko myself. (*Pause.*) It's just you in there, eh?

ROSE. You keep asking me that!

CLIFF. And you keep telling me yes, but look, Rose, I understand and it's late and I'm double-parked out there and if you got company tonight I could always drop in another time and I guess it just wasn't meant to be tonight.

ROSE. You think I invite people up here?

CLIFF. You invited me up here.

ROSE. Everybody always throws stuff back in your face.

CLIFF. Hi. We're everybody.

ROSE. (*Slamming the door.*) Everytime!

CLIFF. Ever slam this door on the museum guy?

ROSE. I never took the curator up here!

CLIFF. Yeah, he brings you down in the cellar to talk about mankind!

ROSE. Why don't you get some quarters, dimes, and nickels and go choke a phonebooth!

CLIFF. You bleed for mankind! but when a real live man's at your door, you give him splinters in the nose!

(*Long pause.* ROSE *opens the door a little.*)

CLIFF. I was halfway home, flat-out on 95, the road empty, radio goin baby o baby, and I notice my blinker winkin at me and the rig threaded a jughandle with a mind of its own, and I don't know if I paid the tolls or ran red lights or stopped at STOP signs or ran over a dog, but I'm back like a homing pigeon.

(*Pause.* ROSE *shuts the door. Pause. She undoes the chain, opens the door a little, looks in the hallway. No* CLIFF. *She opens the door wide. No* CLIFF. *She goes into the hallway Right.* CLIFF, *hiding hallway Left rushes into the room and locks* ROSE *out.*)

ROSE. Hey!
CLIFF. Who's there?
ROSE. Open this door!
CLIFF. I'm not that kind of guy.
ROSE. Cliff!
    (*He opens the door.* ROSE *enters scratching.*)
ROSE. See what you did!
CLIFF. Sorry.
ROSE. You always say you're sorry!
CLIFF. I'm always sorry for something around you.
ROSE. Talk low!
CLIFF. Sorry.
ROSE. The old lady's all over the wall tonight.
CLIFF. What's to listen to?
ROSE. Me.
CLIFF. But you're alone.
ROSE. I really hate this. Always where I can't reach.

CLIFF. Let me.

ROSE. You caused 'em! You kid around too much!

CLIFF. You don't know how to itch. Let me show you.

ROSE. What do you know? You never had hives.

CLIFF. Hey, I know a bee with hives.

ROSE. You never stop.

CLIFF. Let me teach you. We'll start from scratch. Easy. Gentle. See? How's that?

ROSE. More in the middle.

CLIFF. Eh?

ROSE. Up alittle.

CLIFF. Better?

ROSE. Harder.

CLIFF. Was I right?

ROSE. Mmmm.

CLIFF. Admit it.

ROSE. Mmmm.

CLIFF. Mmmm. What do you do when you're alone?

ROSE. Doorknob.

CLIFF. What's nicer?

ROSE. I don't know.

CLIFF. Don't know. You smile and the world goes away. *(He kisses her head.)*

ROSE. Don't, ok?

CLIFF. You bring it out in me.

ROSE. I'm not trying to.

CLIFF. Then why'd you get all specialed up?

ROSE. Just washed my hair, that's all.

CLIFF. Ribbon in your hair.

ROSE. Really?

CLIFF. Expecting company?

ROSE. No.

CLIFF. Going someplace?

ROSE. Bed.

CLIFF. Bed?

ROSE. It's late.

CLIFF. All specialed up for the dead cactus to look at?

ROSE. It's not really that dead.

CLIFF. Does this corner of your mouth know what the other's up to?

ROSE. Don't, please?

CLIFF. Hey, I'm sorry, but I'm not, see, because I can't get over how this lip is so different from this one, or how your cheek pulls back the skin and all of a sudden there's a smile, and I look, it's there, I blink, it's gone, and everytime I see it, it's always the first time, see, so I'm sorry, but I'm not, because I want it, I want it in my coffee in the morning, I want it in my afternoon beer, and I want it in my nighttimes, I want it, and if the door's locked, and the curtain's drawn, if one mouth found another quiet and sweet and wonderful, maybe it's not as good as money in the bank, but it can't be as bad as smoking two packs a day, so I'm sorry, but I'm not because I could be wherever I want right now, but I'm here and you're there, and all the travellin I want to do is from here to there...

ROSE. *(pause)* So how've you been?

CLIFF. Fine, thanks.

ROSE. Good.

CLIFF. And you?

ROSE. Fine, thank you.

CLIFF. Rosie, do you believe in life before death?

ROSE. You mean life *after* death.

CLIFF. No. I mean life now, here, tonight.

ROSE. Shhh! That was her just then!

CLIFF. *(To the wall.)* But what should we do with the body?

ROSE. Shhh! *(She pushes him on the bed, his face lands on the pillow.)*

CLIFF. That your hair that scent?

ROSE. No. Perfume.

CLIFF. Perfume?

ROSE. Like it?

CLIFF. Mmmmm.

ROSE. It's imported.

CLIFF. Beautiful.

ROSE. From New Orleans.

CLIFF. You always splash on perfume before you hit the sack?

ROSE. Makes me dream.

CLIFF. Of what?

ROSE. Things.

CLIFF. Things.

ROSE. Sniff.

CLIFF. Mmmmm.

ROSE. What's it remind you of?

CLIFF. Lug nuts.

ROSE. No.

CLIFF. Jerkins.

ROSE. No, sniff again. *(She squirts his eyes.)* It's called Tooch Mwa. I get twenty percent off at the Five and Dime.

CLIFF. Beautiful.

ROSE. What's it remind you of?

CLIFF. Bullshit.

ROSE. *(Long pause.)* You always ruin everything.

CLIFF. Brenda, did she wear lipstick to bed too?

ROSE. Brenda?

CLIFF. Yeah, you know, eighth floor Brenda.

ROSE. What's wrong?

CLIFF. You know, die-in-the-snow Brenda.

ROSE. I don't understand you.

CLIFF. How come the bed's all messed up?

ROSE. I was sleeping.

CLIFF. In a sweater.

ROSE. I was cold.

CLIFF. And lipstick? and perfume?

ROSE. So what?

CLIFF. Hair fixed and ribbon?

ROSE. So what?

CLIFF. SO WHAT! I do a u-turn. So what!

ROSE. Will you lower your voice?

CLIFF. Why'd you take so long to answer the door?

ROSE. It takes me awhile to wake up.

CLIFF. I'm in the hall, ask if you're alone, I get a big stall-out, hear funny things goin on in here ...

ROSE. Shh! Mrs. Mancuso!

CLIFF. Fuck that glass-ear bitch! *(He kicks the wall.)* Crazy bitch.

ROSE. You talking to me?

CLIFF. How should I know? Around here you open your mouth, you don't know where a set of ears might be.

ROSE. Are you drunk?

CLIFF. You got somebody in there, don't you?

ROSE. What?

CLIFF. C'mon, c'mon, you got somebody in the closet, don't you?

ROSE. No.

CLIFF. Move.

ROSE. No.

CLIFF. Look, Rose, I don't give a shit, understand?

ROSE. I don't know what happened to you.

CLIFF. You stash some idiot twerp and then let me pour my guts out?

ROSE. You must be crazy.

CLIFF. Me, not you, me!

ROSE. Will you lower your voice?

CLIFF. Sure. How's this? Move.

ROSE. I don't know you now.

CLIFF. Tell him to come out.

ROSE. Who?

CLIFF. C'mon, c'mon, c'mon!

ROSE. There's nobody!

CLIFF. How come I don't believe you?

ROSE. I don't care if you don't believe me.

CLIFF. Would you care if I rip the door off the hinges?

ROSE. You have to go. I have to go to work.

CLIFF. After midnight? What's at the Five and Ten? the whacko rush?

ROSE. Goodnight.

CLIFF. Tell chickenass to come out so I could say goodnight.

ROSE. There's nobody.

CLIFF. Here chick, chick, chick, chick, chick . . .

ROSE. Why can't you just believe me?

CLIFF. Because everywhere I go I find I been there before. —MOVE!

ROSE. You just have to believe me.

CLIFF. Do me a favor?

ROSE. What?

CLIFF. Open the door and show me nobody's there?

ROSE. I wouldn't lie.

CLIFF. Noooo, not you!

ROSE. There's nobody!

CLIFF. Show me! Look, Rose, I'm not gonna throw no hands. If you got another man, what's that to me?

ROSE. Don't ever say you're not like them!

CLIFF. Like them! I am them! (*He smashes the crate against the wall.*) Who'd you think I was? Johnny Gallant on a white horse ready to pick up the tab for every dipshit that ever got a rod for you? (CLIFF *opens the closet. Inside, men's sweaters on hangers. Long pause.*)

Nice selection. (*Pulling a sweater off a hanger.*) Got anything in a turtleneck?

ROSE. They're Brenda's.

CLIFF. And the one you got on, that Brenda's too?

ROSE. No, this one's yours.

CLIFF. So when's mine get to hang with these, eh, Brenda?

ROSE. What?

CLIFF. When you ask some other asshole for his, eh, Brenda?

ROSE. No.

CLIFF. What was this guy's name, eh, Brenda? (*Drops sweater on floor, kicks it at* ROSE.)

ROSE. Don't!

CLIFF. Was it true love?

ROSE. Please don't. (*She retrieves the kicked sweater.*)

CLIFF. (*Throwing a sweater at her.*) You dippy fuckin gooney-bird!

ROSE. Please?

CLIFF. And what was this guy's name? (*Throwing a sweater at her.*) Was he a truck driver or screwdriver? And this one with the little reindeers and snowflakes! Was it meant to be? (*Throwing a sweater.*)

ROSE. STOP IT!

CLIFF. Did this one die in the snow for you? (*Throwing a sweater.*)

ROSE. Stop it! Stop it!

CLIFF. And what was this guy's name, eh, Sister Rose? (*Throwing a sweater.*) And this one? How long did this one last? (*Throwing a sweater.*)

ROSE. Killing the birds!

CLIFF. I always get the fuckin loonies.

ROSE. Legs snapped like straws!

CLIFF. Fuckin birds.

ROSE. Wings flapping in the water!

CLIFF. What a fuckin Jonah! (*About to throw a sweater, but seeing* ROSE *frozen in the image of the birds, he drops it, begins to exit.*)

ROSE. Mangled and bloody and broken in the water. Beaks alittle open. Still. And one with the eye open. Making a baby sound. Eye open making a baby sound. Its breast beating hard. Hard. Hard. Hard. Hard. And less hard. And less hard. And not so hard. And not so hard. And alittle less hard. And then alittle bit. And alittle bit. And then very little. And soft. And soft. And very soft. And then nothing. Soft. The feathers. Soft. The breast. Soft. The eyes. Soft. Making a baby sound. A little sound. Soft. (*She imitates this sound.*)

CLIFF. (*Re-entering.*) Rose, get off the floor.

ROSE. Look what they did! Look!

CLIFF. Rose, get up.

ROSE. Animals! How could you punish them? You can't make the birds come alive again!

CLIFF. Rose, up!

ROSE. I don't want to go there!

CLIFF. (*Slapping her. She backs away from him.*) Rose, I'm sorry, I'm so sorry. I never hit a woman before. Except her. Once. When I got home a day early, caught 'em, I'm sorry.

ROSE. No needle!

CLIFF. What needle? I don't have a . . .

ROSE. I don't want to sleep. I want to run out in the street and scream, They killed the birds! They killed the birds! They stoned the birds! And nobody cares! Nobody!

CLIFF. Rose . . .

ROSE. So I have to care for everybody . . .

CLIFF. Shhh! Ok, ok, shhh!

ROSE. And I asked the zoo guard where they buried the birds, and he said they didn't bury them and I said

CLIFF. No, just standing still forever.

ROSE. Once I watched the cranes standing so still in the water when the sun was going down. So still. But more alive than anything moving. And so graceful. And beautiful. And I watched the last of the light brush up against their feathers, their pure feathers, and edge 'em with a dandylion glow, like a halo, gold and white. Wings spread, standing like magnificent angels in the dark water, and how they stepped so graceful! like they thought about each step! And it was like being in church, and I thought I heard music, and I wanted to sing or pray or I-don't-know-what . . . because if you look at them in a certain light, if you look at them and let them inside you, it makes you graceful and alive and beautiful too.

CLIFF. Hey, Rose, you ever hear of the laws of nature? Here ya go: If you're a bird, right, and your folks didn't beget no off-spring, chances are, you won't either.

ROSE. But if the parents didn't beget offspring . . .

CLIFF. Right! Now what do you suppose comes down when the zookeepers go home? You think them birds stand around counting each other's fleas? Hey, the place turns into a regular Sodom and Gomorrah. And before you blink, you got a couple eggs on your hands. Long eggs, you know, to accommodate them stilts.

ROSE. How many could they have?

CLIFF. Hey, maybe five, six at a clip.

ROSE. That many?

CLIFF. Well it's alittle outside my field of endeavor, but hey, if you're dealing with hustling independents, maybe seven or eight eggs.

ROSE. How long's it take?

CLIFF. You're talkin acouple weeks.

ROSE. More than that.

CLIFF. Alright, so you get stuck with union birds and they drag it out acouple months. The whole foul-up's them legs. I mean, hey, if they had normal legs, that's one thing, but when you got to grow legs this long for a body this big, hey, you're in a ditch and a half, unless of course you luck out and get hold of a leg-stretcher.

ROSE. A what?

CLIFF. Leg-stretcher.

ROSE. Never heard of it.

CLIFF. It's an adjustable leg-brace on the end of an eye-screw you turn to stretch things out. I used to haul 'em from the factory in Phoenix to a zoo out Sacramento where they got a big population of birds with stubby legs.

ROSE. Where?

CLIFF. Hey, Sacramento.

ROSE. Any killer crows attack, champ?

CLIFF. You got to see it, Rose—something that escapes when you try and nail it down. I want you to be there when we come round that mountain and there's nothing between you and a thousand foot fall but a guard rail made of popsickle sticks, and you catch wiff of a batch of air sprinkled with salt and turn the mountain and the big, deep, wide Pacific Ocean slams you in the old chops and blinds you with a light-flash that makes you dizzy tipsy, and you look around wonderin where you're gonna steal your next breath from . . .

ROSE. It's like you get new eyes, and nothing looks the same . . .

CLIFF. And there it is: colors like nothing you saw before, like some delinquent went nuts with blue finger-paints and smeared 'em as wide and deep and far as the eyeball can roll . . .

ROSE. So pretty, it scares you it might go away . . .

CLIFF. And you're up in that truck rounding the mountain and you're awake like never before, like after a life of catnaps, and you sing and make happy silly noises because there's nobody there . . .

ROSE. Nobody, but you don't want it to go to waste . . .

CLIFF. And you crave the sound of a human voice, even your own . . .

ROSE. But you want a voice different from your own to come back to you . . .

CLIFF. And you see cities along the coast . . .

ROSE. Like beads on a necklace . . .

CLIFF. And the breeze finds a way inside you . . .

ROSE. So salty . . .

CLIFF. So fresh . . .

ROSE. You can taste it . . .

CLIFF. And the sun . . .

ROSE. So close . . .

CLIFF. So warm . . .

ROSE. You feel it touch you . . .

CLIFF. Like a hand on your shoulder, that warm . . .

ROSE. And it goes through you . . .

CLIFF. And you're never the same again . . .

ROSE. And you think somehow it happened before . . .

CLIFF. So beautiful . . .

ROSE. So so beautiful . . .

(*Lights fade.*)

*END*

# PROPERTY LIST

## ACT ONE

*Off Right:*
   Six pack Schmidt's beer in brown paper bag

ONSTAGE
*Stage Right:*
   Waste basket
   Cover for bathtub
   Hot plate
   Steam kettle
   Kitchen towel
   Bar of soap
*On Shelves Over Sink:*
   Can of sardines
   Magic Mountain herb tea
   Corn niblets
   Artichoke hearts
   Asparagus tips
   Gherkins
   Fruits and nuts
   Seaweed soup
   Cinnamon sticks
   Bouillon cubes
   Drinking glass
   2 cooking pots
   2 plates

UPSTAGE
*Near Refrigerator:*
   Mop
   Broom
   Dust pan

*In Refrigerator:*
    Bowl with 4 hardboiled eggs
    1 stalk of old celery
    ½ filled bottle cranberry juice
    Box of baking soda
    1 stick of butter
*Near Closet:*
    Fruit crate (reinforced)

STAGE LEFT
*On Shelves Up Left:*
    Dying ivy plant
    Dying cactus plant
    Make up mirror
    Hand lotion
    Lipstick
    Perfume in spray bottle
    Hair brush

*Down Left:*
    Trunk
    Suitcase
    Lamp
    Good Housekeeping magazine
    Flower book
    Book with handwritten poem on piece of paper inside book
    Dinosaur pamphlet

## PERSONAL PROPS

ROSE:
  Apartment keys
CLIFF:
  Chewing gum
  Plastic film can with herbal tobacco
  Rolling papers in metal case
  Cigarette lighter
  Matches
  Pack of Marlboro cigarettes
  Eyedrops

## ACT TWO

Replace fruit crate with breakaway crate

# Also By

# William Mastrosimone

BALALAIKA

CAT'S-PAW

EXTREMITIES

IMAGO

NANAWATAI

A STONE CARVER

TAMER OF HORSES

A TANTALIZING

THE UNDOING

# WHITE BUFFALO
## Don Zolidis

*Drama / 3m, 2f (plus chorus)/ Unit Set*

Based on actual events, WHITE BUFFALO tells the story of the miracle birth of a white buffalo calf on a small farm in southern Wisconsin. When Carol Gelling discovers that one of the buffalo on her farm is born white in color, she thinks nothing more of it than a curiosity. Soon, however, she learns that this is the fulfillment of an ancient prophecy believed by the Sioux to bring peace on earth and unity to all mankind. Her little farm is quickly overwhelmed with religious pilgrims, bringing her into contact with a culture and faith that is wholly unfamiliar to her. When a mysterious businessman offers to buy the calf for two million dollars, Carol is thrown into doubt about whether to profit from the religious beliefs of others or to keep true to a spirituality she knows nothing about.

# ANON
## Kate Robin

*Drama / 2m, 12f / Area*

Anon. follows two couples as they cope with sexual addiction. Trip and Allison are young and healthy, but he's more interested in his abnormally large porn collection than in her. While they begin to work through both of their own sexual and relationship hang-ups, Trip's parents are stuck in the roles they've been carving out for years in their dysfunctional marriage. In between scenes with these four characters, 10 different women, members of a support group for those involved with individuals with sex addiction issues, tell their stories in monologues that are alternately funny and harrowing..

In addition to Anon., Robin's play What They Have was also commissioned by South Coast Repertory. Her plays have also been developed at Manhattan Theater Club, Playwrights Horizons, New York Theatre Workshop, The Eugene O'Neill Theater Center's National Playwrights Conference, JAW/West at Portland Center Stage and Ensemble Studio Theatre. Television and film credits include "Six Feet Under" (writer/supervising producer) and "Coming Soon." Robin received the 2003 Princess Grace Statuette for playwriting and is an alumna of New Dramatists.

# BLUE YONDER
Kate Aspengren

*Dramatic Comedy / Monolgues and scenes*
*12f (can be performed with as few as 4 with doubling) / Unit Set*

A familiar adage states, "Men may work from sun to sun, but women's work is never done." In Blue Yonder, the audience meets twelve mesmerizing and eccentric women including a flight instructor, a firefighter, a stuntwoman, a woman who donates body parts, an employment counselor, a professional softball player, a surgical nurse professional baseball player, and a daredevil who plays with dynamite among others. Through the monologues, each woman examines her life's work and explores the career that she has found. Or that has found her.

# TREASURE ISLAND
Ken Ludwig

*All Groups / Adventure / 10m, 1f (doubling) / Areas*
Based on the masterful adventure novel by Robert Louis Stevenson, *Treasure Island* is a stunning yarn of piracy on the tropical seas. It begins at an inn on the Devon coast of England in 1775 and quickly becomes an unforgettable tale of treachery and mayhem featuring a host of legendary swashbucklers including the dangerous Billy Bones (played unforgettably in the movies by Lionel Barrymore), the sinister two-timing Israel Hands, the brassy woman pirate Anne Bonney, and the hideous form of evil incarnate, Blind Pew. At the center of it all are Jim Hawkins, a 14-year-old boy who longs for adventure, and the infamous Long John Silver, who is a complex study of good and evil, perhaps the most famous hero-villain of all time. Silver is an unscrupulous buccaneer-rogue whose greedy quest for gold, coupled with his affection for Jim, cannot help but win the heart of every soul who has ever longed for romance, treasure and adventure.